LUCY MY LOVE

A HISTORICAL ROMANCE

BY

DIANA BASKERVYLE-GLEGG

Matador
9 Priory Business Park,
Wistow Road, Kibworth Beauchamp,
Leicestershire. LE8 0RX
Tel: (+44) 116 279 2299
Fax: (+44) 116 279 2277
Email: books@troubador.co.uk
Web: www.troubador.co.uk/matador

ISBN 9781783060252

British Library Cataloguing in Publication Data.
A catalogue record for this book is available from the
British Library.

Typeset by Troubador Publishing Ltd, Leicester, UK

Matador is an imprint of Troubador Publishing Ltd

For Richard Gray

CONTENTS

PART 2.

PREFACE

This is the story of my husband's great aunt Lucy, who lived at Baskerville Hall, near Knutsford, Cheshire. Baskerville Hall, which features in this book, was at some stage, renamed Withington Hall, and was the home of my husband since childhood. This house was rebuilt in the Regency period, in 1795 on the site of the original house, which was probably built in the Tudor period, during the reign of Queen Elizabeth, when so many country houses were built, but I like to think that there had been a house built on the site earlier than that.

The Baskerville-Gleggs had a tradition of being Masters of the Hunt, the local hunt being at Tarporley near Crewe, and it is a tradition that every year they have a dinner at the Swan Hotel. My husband had a painting by Terence Cuneo of this dinner, and I still have it in my possession.

He had our dining room in our house in London painted in the same colour green as that on the walls of the dining room at the Swan – surely a piece of nostalgia. Eventually my husband had to sell Withington Hall, sometime in the 1960s, because it needed a new roof. Cost – £150,000. Eventually it was sold to a scrap merchant, pulled down and rebuilt in the same style as the original house, and it is still there today. My husband would never return there because it had too many memories. (see illustration).

INTRODUCTION

Discovering more about my husband's family has been a fascinating exercise, and the more I have researched, the more intriguing it has become. So much so, that when I came across his great aunt Lucy Baskerville-Glegg on the Internet, (who, in real life lived until the 1900s), I decided to make her the heroine of my tale.

Lord Anstruther, the hero, was a baronet from Drayton Maltravers, a small village in the county of Lincolnshire, and has been inspired by a real life baronet named Robert Carnegie Jervis, who eventually marries our heroine; but I have been unable to trace the location in which he lived. There is, therefore, a mixture of fact and fiction in this book, which is, nevertheless, an authentic portrait of life amongst the aristocracy in the eighteenth century, with a plot which I hope will satisfy my readers.

Lucy Charlotte, according to the entry on the Internet, lived in the middle of the nineteenth century, but I have placed her in the late eighteenth century, because I wished my characters to travel by coach instead of by train, in order to give the book a more period flavour. Indeed, so important have the journeys become in the unfolding of the plot, that they have adopted an identity all of their own. In fact travelling by coach and horses in the eighteenth century was a hazardous affair; the coach might overturn on severely rutted roads, which were always crowded with packhorses; it might be accosted by highwaymen armed with pistols, or a wheel might drop off, causing an accident and requiring a repair which might take several hours. One could in fact, sustain an injury in the course of one's journey, which could have lasting effects.

Every aristocratic family possessed at least one coach and a team of horses. Country houses would have stables for the horses and a coach house for the coach. Phaetons were considered suitable only for short distances and barouche-landaus (closed carriages) were far more desirable if the weather was inclement and were used for long distance travel, and usually emblazoned with the family's coat of arms. The coachman, described as having flaxen curls and dressed in a cocked hat, was a status symbol, and was considered necessary to all members of the landowning classes. The 'dickie', a seat used by the valet, was at the rear of the coach.

Medicine of course, was still relatively basic, decades before the advent of the smallpox vaccine introduced by Edward Jenner, and was not at all the panacea it is today, something which is highlighted by Lucy's illness and the danger of mortality, in an age more than one hundred and fifty years before the introduction of antibiotics.

Furthermore daughters of the landed aristocracy did not have employment at that time and Lucy, who would be considered un-emancipated today in our feminist world, lived at home with her parents, developing skills in music, singing and art. The novels of Jane Austen bear testimony to this. A favourite pastime to while away the hours was stitching, anything from canvas embroidery to stumpwork.

The Baskerville estates consisted of the squire's own land, an estate of some two thousand acres, including a farm and a large deer park, as well as tenanted farms from which he collected rents. It was these rents that were such a lucrative source of income, although originally Lord Anstruther's fortune had been founded on the lucrative industry of lacemaking. The squire at that time would have the responsibility of looking after the farmstead and the numerous farm buildings which were dotted about the estate. To help him he would have a factor and bailiff as well as labourers.

Sir John Baskerville-Glegg, the father of Lucy, the heroine of this tale, was the Member of Parliament for the area of Cheshire in which he lived. Although he paid lip service to elections, his was a shire seat secured by virtue of his position in the county. He and his wife Isabella had six children, two boys and four girls, including Lucy and Jessica, while their sons were called Edmund and John.

It was customary at this time to entertain large numbers of guests at house parties of up to eighty guests. Not surprisingly the house they lived in had more than seventy bedrooms and a large army of servants to look after the guests, as well as the family. A gentleman would bring his own valet when he stayed with friends, and a lady her own maid. Staff in country houses consisted of parlourmaids and valets as well as kitchen staff. Each lady brought her maid, who looked after her clothes, laying them out on her bed each morning and evening. My husband recollected that when he lived at Baskerville Hall, his parents employed a boy whose sole job it was to light the oil lamps every evening throughout the house. The staff slept in the attics and an entire community slept under one roof.

England in the late eighteenth century was on the brink of revolution, both social and economic. The Industrial Revolution, contemporaneous as it was with the agrarian revolution, brought untold wealth to all those factory owners, but also hardship to the rural poor. It created a new social class of wealthy manufacturers who established themselves as a powerful force in politics in the nineteenth century. It brought about the growth of large cities, and large scale migration from the country to the cities where work could be found. This was the social phenomenon portrayed so well in the novels of Charles Dickens.

Squires such as our hero continued to prosper, but it was the rich factory owners who built large mansions out of the proceeds from their enterprises, many of which have either been pulled down or reduced in size because of the expense of keeping them up.

A gentleman could employ up to thirty five gardeners, some of whom worked in the walled kitchen garden, which was devoted to fruit and vegetables as well as flowers for cutting for the house. Its sun-kissed walls were home to quantities of peaches, apples and pears, as well as enclosing a large supply of vegetables. In addition special sunken pits existed for the cultivation of pineapples.

Glasshouses were heated cheaply by boilers fired by a plentiful supply of coal. There was, however, a heavy tax on glass at this time, and all but the wealthy were able to afford glasshouses. It was not until 1831 that this tax, instituted in 1696, was repealed.

At the time of our story, the labouring classes lived in pitiful conditions, barely scraping a wage large enough to live on. Many of them lived in hovels with walls of mud, but it has to be said that our hero managed to raise his tenants' cottages up to a level of comfort almost unknown on other estates. The profits made from the old established family lace industry provided the funds for improvements to these houses. Improvements in agriculture, brought about by the introduction of enclosed fields in the 1770s, also contributed to the increased prosperity of landowners.

In the latter part of the century however, a series of bad harvests had made several landowners bankrupt, and Peregrine our hero, had himself been forced to sell some of his land, as well as some of the trees in his woodland, in order to pay his debts.

What are we to think of the chief characters in this book? Lucy Charlotte has been portrayed as headstrong, determined, loyal and a woman ahead of her age. Peregrine was sensitive, unusually emotional for a man, and easily wounded. And yet they complemented each other perfectly.

CHAPTER ONE

SETTING THE SCENE

The Baskerville-Gleggs had lived at Baskerville Hall near Knutsford since the eighteenth century, and were an old landed family who had held lands in Cheshire since the days of Sir John Baskerville in 1265. It was said that the Baskervilles originally came from Normandy, and that Baudry de Baskerville was the chief archer in William's army, responsible for killing Harold by shooting him in the eye with an arrow, but this may be the stuff of legends, handed down through the ages. At any rate one thing is certain, that while the Baskervilles originated from Shropshire, the Gleggs came from Cheshire, and If you go to Wirral today, you will see the Glegg Arms as a sign of their importance.

A country estate would consist of the squire's own land, an estate of some two thousand acres including a large deer park, a home farm and numerous tenanted farms from which he would collect rents. It was these rents which were such a lucrative source of income, in spite of the fact that the squire had the responsibility of looking after his tenants, and the numerous farm buildings which were dotted about the estate, including the tenants' cottages.

Sir John Baskerville-Glegg, the father of Lucy, heroine of this novel, was the Member of Parliament for the area of Cheshire in which he lived. Although he paid lip service to elections, his was a shire seat secured by virtue of his position in the county. He and his wife Isabella had eight children, one of which, the eldest, was Lucy, the other, Susan. It was customary at this time to entertain large numbers of guests at house parties of up to eighty guests. Not surprisingly the house had more than seventy bedrooms and a large army of servants to look after the guests, together with their own valets and ladies' maids, who all slept in the attics. Besides the usual servants, there was the ubiquitous butler, who performed a variety of functions from answering the front door to visitors, to waiting at table. My husband used to tell me that a boy was employed for no other reason than to light the numerous oil lamps in the house, for not many houses had electricity. A lady's maid would see to her mistress's clothes, laying them out on her bed each morning and evening. Her mistress would, of course, have indicated which garments she would wear. She was responsible for pressing and keeping them in immaculate condition. One might say that an entire community lived under one roof.

According to the official history of the Baskerville-Glegg family, a Mary Baskerville had married Sir William Glegg some time at the beginning of the eighteenth century, thus uniting the two families. History records that William Glegg had been knighted by William III after he had spent the night at Withington Hall – but the date of this event is not known. Portraits of both Sir William Glegg and Mary Baskerville were painted by Sir Peter Lely, the fashionable portrait painter of the day, and were in our possession, before being passed to my stepson, Major General John Baskervyle-Glegg. Portraits of course were a valuable source of information on the period, especially about costume, and especially when they show scenes of the family's estate in the background.

The principal pastime of a country squire in the eighteenth century was foxhunting, for which sport he kept his own pack of hounds. Often he himself was Master of the Hunt and, dressed in his scarlet hunting coat he cut a dashing figure. Hunting scenes of the period, painted by Stubbs or Thornley, can often be found in country houses today.

CHAPTER TWO

THE DINNER PARTY

In March 1790 the Baskerville-Gleggs, with one of their house parties in residence, were giving a large dinner party, and on the afternoon of the party, Lucy went driving in the Park with her mother, but Lady Baskerville-Glegg was worried. She had invited the Barfords their neighbours to dinner, together with their guest Lord Anstruther, who had long admired her eldest daughter, but Lucy, she thought, was too discriminating, too cerebral, and unlikely, in her present state, to find a suitable husband. Even if Peregrine Anstruther wished to marry Lucy, would she have HIM, one of the best catches she was ever likely to meet? She imagined in her fantasy world, Lucy ensconced at Marningham Hall, Peregrine's country seat, with at least eight children, all beautiful of course, and all likely to marry titled spouses. She was brought up with a start by the grey pony stumbling over a large stone and her attention for the moment at least, was diverted.

She must speak to her on the subject, she thought to herself.

Now would be a good time, before she met Peregrine at the dinner party.

'Lucy,' she said. 'Surely you know that Peregrine adores you.'

'Not at all,' replied Lucy. 'He had never said that he loves me,'

'Well, you can see it in his eyes every time he looks at you,' said Lady Baskerville-Glegg. It is plain to see.'

Not only were the house guests to be present at the dinner, but also their neighbours and friends. Were we to be allowed to see Lord Anstruther Bart. In his dressing room at Barford Park on the eve of the party, we would find him on the horns of a dilemma. Should he wear his yellow embroidered waistcoat or his blue one? Finally he comes to a decision and he chooses the blue one, adjusts his cravat, smoothes his silk frock coat under which his beautiful blue waistcoat is just visible, and surveys himself in the looking glass. He was not displeased with what he saw – he cut a dashing figure, his dark hair liberally powdered and his face, with its aquiline nose, was handsome. He was, he knew, one of the most eligible bachelors in the county of Lincolnshire, and any girl of marriageable age would be pleased to take him as their husband. Tonight, he was well aware, he would meet the two sisters Jessica and Lucy at Baskerville Hall. Lucy the eldest was his favourite, and in his sober moments he thought of her as his ideal bride. What would she say if he were to propose, he wondered? Etiquette of the period forbade him to take any liberties with her person. A formal proposal would have to take place, with himself on bended knee and a ring ready in his pocket. He must choose his moment carefully he decided...

The other guests had already arrived and

were assembled in the drawing room when Peregrine arrived at the Hall that evening in the company of his hosts. They were welcomed by Sir John and Lady Baskerville-Glegg, who shook each guest by the hand, and beckoned to the butler to offer them a drink. A roaring log fire was burning in the huge fireplace- the guests having disposed themselves on the two sofahs before it. Peregrine meanwhile had caught sight of Lucy, who looked radiant in a dress of pale blue satin, with a diamond tiara about her head.

'Have you had a good day's hunting?' she asked, beaming.

'Needless to say,' answered Peregrine, 'the fox got away.'

In a short while the butler announced that dinner was about to be served, whereupon each lady took a gentleman by the arm and was escorted by him into the dining room, where three footmen stood respectfully by.

Peregrine silently marvelled at the spectacle which lay in front of him – a long table on which were set priceless crystal goblets, silver cutlery and beautiful porcelain, all illumined by a chandelier hanging from above adorned with a hundred flickering candles. The feast was considerable, far more than we would eat today - quails' eggs, pheasant, partridge and other meats were served from silver platters, together with a plethora of vegetables of different kinds. Then suddenly, just at the very moment when the chatter of the guests reached it climax, there came the most almighty crash as the chandelier with its hundred burning candles, bounced off the table and fell to the ground, singeing the Aubusson carpet and narrowly missing the head of one of the guests.

Pandemonium followed. The guests hurriedly filed out of the smoke filled room, and it being quite out of the question for them to continue their meal in the dining room, Lady Baskerville-Glegg ordered the rest of the meal to be served in the Painted Parlour. Down in the servants' hall, there was much conjecture as what had caused the chandelier to break loose from its chain, each one blaming the other for the unfortunate incident. Undaunted by the catastrophe, the guests sat down, all except Lucy that is, who had disappeared from the scene, while everyone else enjoyed liberal helpings from the three tiered jellies. After the meal, the gentlemen adjourned to play that most traditional of games – billiards, while the ladies retired to the drawing room to gossip, Presently Lucy re-appeared and sang 'Ye bonnie banks and braes', while her sister Jessica played.

The next morning Peregrine took Lucy driving in the park, in a phaeton borrowed from his hosts. She said nothing of her sudden disappearance the night before, but told him of the trees her father had planted, and that he had employed the landscape gardener Humphry Repton to landscape the park, while Peregrine made suitable admiring comments.

After that morning he saw little of her, except briefly on the hunting field, and in early

March, when the hunting season had ended, he arranged to depart for Lincolnshire. Before he left however, he had one important task, to ask for Lucy's hand in marriage.

CHAPTER THREE

SIR JOHN BASKERVILLE-GLEGG
GOES TO LONDON

Meanwhile at the beginning of the week after the chaotic dinner party, Sir John prepared to depart for London, where Parliament was re-assembling after the Easter recess. The horse drawn carriage clattered briskly down the drive of Baskerville Hall, as Sir John resigned himself to the long and arduous journey ahead. Constant changes of horses were necessary (every twelve miles) which was irritating for they slowed down the journey considerably, but it would have been inadvisable to overwork the horses and to drive them to do longer journeys than was good for them. Inns were dispersed along the route, where fresh horses could be hired, the ostler taking the horses to the stables where they were fed and watered. In all there were twelve changes of horses to be accomplished before they reached London. Eventually they arrived at the town of Ware, on the outskirts of a city considerably smaller than it is today. Arriving at the inn at Ware, a small town in Hertfordshire, Sir John dismounted and the coachman led the horses to the stables, where they were released from the shafts by the ostler.

'Tinkerbell, the grey mare, needs a new shoe,' said the coachman.

'Two blacksmiths will arrive on the morrow, and this will be attended to,' replied the ostler.

'In that case,' said the coachman, 'all four horses can be attended to.'

The next morning, at nine o'clock prompt, the blacksmiths arrived and the horses were shod, the molten shoes applied to their hooves. The coach then departed for London. Finally they reached the rural village of Hampstead and then on to Bloomsbury, where Sir John's house was situated.

London, capital of the British Isles, noisy,

bustling and dirty and yet, despite this, the hub of the Universe. 'If a man is tired of London he is tired of Life,' said Dr. Johnson- in his day filled with coffee houses where agreeable conversation could take place. With this thought in mind, Sir John prepared to enjoy himself and after taking tea in his study, which was served by Monson the butler, he prepared to depart for his Club.

'What news here, Monson?'

'Mrs Fothergill called this morning Sir, and left her card. She said she would return.'

'Did she say what her business was?' asked Sir John. He would know soon enough. Mrs Fothergill had promised to return the next day. He suspected that she had come about the Foundling Hospital of which he was a patron.

After tea Sir John walked down to Golden Lane, to the Fanshawe Club, where he hoped he would find some interesting company with whom to converse. Unlike womenfolk, who were inclined to talk of nothing but hats and their daughters, his friends would discuss politics, one of his favourite subjects. On this particular occasion he found the assembled company engrossed in conversation about Pitt the Younger and his shortcomings.

Next morning, attired in frock coat and top hat, he attended the opening of Parliament, always a colourful spectacle and an impressive ceremony, at which the ageing King George III would arrive in his gilded State Coach. The ceremony over, he and his fellow Members were given a lavish lunch in Westminster Hall at which various Members gave a speech.

Then he travelled to Vauxhall Gardens in his sedan chair, and booked himself into a performance of 'The Rivals' by Richard Brinsley Sheridan, a foremost playwright of his day.

'Mrs Fothergill to see you Sir,' said Monson the butler, as he was attending to his letters the next morning.

'Show her in,' said Sir John.

Mrs Fothergill, a statuesque figure of

uncertain age, walked into his study and sat down. She was often much given to parlance about nothing in particular, but on this occasion she had come on important business.

'I've come about the Foundling Hospital,' said Mrs Fothergill, drawing a deep breath. She knew only too well that Sir John was not exactly liberal with his money.

Sir John stroked his chin thoughtfully. He would have to go to his bank for such a large amount of money. Indeed he wondered if he even had access to that amount at that precise moment.

'I will do my best,' he said. 'I am returning to Cheshire next week for a few days but I will do my best meanwhile.'

Sir John returned to Cheshire the following week, fifteen thousand pounds poorer than when he had set out, but satisfied that he had played his part in saving the Foundling Hospital from extinction.

CHAPTER FOUR

THE OUTING AND THE PROPOSAL

The afternoon before he left for Lincolnshire, he called at the Hall and was let in through the front door by Carter the butler.

'Miss Lucy is upstairs in her apartment my Lord.'

Peregrine bounded up the stairs, but his attention was caught by the sound of voices in a corridor – strange, unfamiliar voices that he had never heard before. He determined to investigate and, knocking on the door whence the sounds had come, he entered. The strangest scene greeted him; a nursemaid was reading to a pallid child in a wheelchair. He wore callipers on his legs and looked pained.

'I am so sorry to disturb you,' said Peregrine and, confused by what he had seen, hurriedly withdrew. Who was this child he had seen in the nursery, he wondered?

He said nothing about the strange scene he had witnessed when he finally encountered Lucy in the library. Her head immersed in a book, she looked up as soon as he entered.

'What are you reading?' asked Peregrine curiously.

'The Castle of Otranto by Mrs Radcliffe,' replied Lucy.

Peregrine shuddered. He disliked Gothic novels with their overworked sentimentalism, but he recognised that they were extremely popular with ladies because of their content which was charged with emotion of the worst possible kind. Remembering the package, which she had discovered when walking across the hall earlier that afternoon, Lucy was blushing as he took her hand. She had opened the package and found the gloves. The cards, it seemed, were on the table.

'Lucy,' said Peregrine earnestly, but nevertheless with hesitation in his voice. 'This may not be an appropriate time to talk about this subject but I wanted to ask you a question before I leave for Lincolnshire. He drew a deep breath and then continued.

'Will you do me the honour of becoming my wife?' It had taken all his courage to ask this question and now he awaited the answer trembling with fear.

'Peregrine,' replied Lucy. 'You know that I have strong feelings for you, but I cannot at the moment accept your proposal, and in time I will tell you the reason why.'

Peregrine sat down and put his head in his hands. It had taken all his courage to propose, and having done so, he was bitterly disappointed at the reply. The atmosphere in the library was charged with emotion. Lucy, for once in her life, had lost her composure, and was near to tears.

'Take my arm and we will go and join your parents in the drawing room,' said the suitor, determined to put on a brave face, and to show the world that he was made of stern stuff.

Nevertheless he was destined to return home a disappointed man.

CHAPTER FIVE

PEREGRINE RETURNS HOME
AND GIVES A BALL

It was nearly the end of March and a cold wind was blowing as Peregrine set off for Lincolnshire. A watery sun bravely attempted to burst through the clouds as the carriage sped down the drive of Barford Hall. He knew the route, across the Pennines, over the Peaks of Derbyshire, passing through Congleton and Macclesfield on the way. In the distance he could see Cross Peak, the highest peak in the Pennines. There were the usual nightly stops at uncomfortable inns with their indifferent food, Some nights he stayed with friends, a welcome respite from the inns he disliked so much. By early evening on the third day, he turned in through the gates of Marningham Hall, the large Palladian mansion with its flanking wings, which had been his home since childhood. He had mixed feelings about this house. It was unwieldy in its monumental size, which intensified his feelings of loneliness. Nevertheless, he was determined to remain in the family home, with or without a wife.

Once inside the house, he felt more at ease, and ordered supper to be brought to his apartment. The next morning he awoke to the sound of church bells from the church across the drive. Well, he decided, he would not attend church today. Instead he would plan his next house party, and hold a ball; forty five guests who lived some distance away, were invited to spend the night with him. Those who lived nearby had no need of overnight hospitality. In all one hundred guests were invited, and then the list grew larger – one hundred became one hundred and fifteen, and then he had to call a halt. Already he knew that he would have to engage extra staff to cope with the swollen numbers. Each guest brought either a valet or lady's maid. Lucy and Jessica, were as might be expected, on the guest list, and their mother acted as chaperone.

As might be expected, Peregrine knew almost everyone in the county, and they knew him. He had attended their balls, their parties and their dinners. He had filled the dance cards of aspiring females, chatted to their mamas, and generally made himself as charming as he possibly could.

The night of the ball arrived, and the kitchen was buzzing with activity. All the salads and sweetmeats had been prepared and taken up to the dining room, where a whole dressed pig lay resplendent on the dining room table. There was an air of intense excitement in the house.

The receiving line at the entrance to the ballroom consisted of Peregrine, his sister Caroline and his brother Tristram. Champagne was flowing and a lively orchestra was playing the popular tunes of the day. The orchestra struck up first a quadrille and then a polka and the floor was filled with the swirling dresses of the ladies, and Lucy, with her dark hair and flashing eyes, looked particularly stunning. She and her sister were dressed as shepherdesses, as fancy dress was the order of the day. Peregrine himself was dressed as a dragon, and his brother a serpent. They both looked strangely surreal in their outfits.

Lady Airlie arrived with her two daughters Caroline and Charlotte, then Lord Barchester.

'Lord Barchester', intoned the Master of Ceremonies, as his lordship shook hands with Peregrine and his brother Tristram. A glass of

Madeira was handed to all the guests. The dancing began and the dance cards began to fill up. Peregrine, to his chagrin, was only allowed one dance with Lucy. Her dance card had soon filled up as she was so popular. The guests tucked into the sumptuous supper – the dressed pig and a variety of salads. At two am. carriages began to arrive at the porte cochère, and the guests bid farewell to their host, thanking him for a wonderful evening. Peregrine went to bed well satisfied with the occasion. His only regret was that he had only managed to have one dance with his beloved Lucy.

⁂

The next morning Peregrine awoke late and looked out of the window. There had been a steady drizzle during the night and the ground was soaked. He arrived downstairs to find not a shred of evidence of the previous night's revelries. The staff had cleared everything away and all was in order. Lucy and her sister did not descend until midday and were full of praise for the ball. 'I have not attended such a splendid ball for ages,' declared Lucy. He words were echoed by her sister. The girls and their mother departed after lunch, long after the rest of the guests, saying that their hosts must return to Cheshire without too much delay.

CHAPTER SIX

THREE MONTHS LATER

At the beginning of June, an opportunity arose for Peregrine to return to Baskerville Hall, but under the most unhappy of circumstances. One afternoon, while he was entertaining friends in the drawing room, Carter the butler brought a message for him on a silver salver. It was from Lady Baskerville-Glegg to say that Lucy had been taken seriously ill and would he come at once. Yet another journey, he thought wearily, and climbed the stairs to his room; a family portrait - his grandfather- gazed down on him with an even more enigmatic expression than usual. He instructed his valet to pack some clothes, and once again he was to make the arduous journey across the Pennines to Baskerville Hall. It was nightfall by the time they started their journey, and the stars were shining brightly in the sky.

They drove through the night, changing horses several times on the way, and only stopped briefly at an inn on the second night, as Peregrine was anxious to reach his beloved's bedside as quickly as possible. Reaching the Hall again by early evening, Peregrine saw that the knocker on the door had been dismantled, in order not to disturb the patient, but the door was already open for him. On the stairs he encountered the doctor, a solemn looking man with greying hair.

'How is she?' asked Peregrine anxiously.

'The prognosis is not good,' said the doctor gloomily. 'I doubt she will last the night.'

As soon as he heard this news, Peregrine was beside himself with grief, and quickened his step, rushing swiftly to the invalid's bedside.

He found her languishing on the pillows, her face a deathly pallor, with the telltale scars of the pox spoiling her lovely countenance.

'Lucy my dear,' said Peregrine softly. 'Listen to me. A miracle will happen and you will recover.'

Then a miracle did indeed happen, and one night, after five days, Lucy opened her eyes. She looked wan and drawn but managed a whisper. At least she was alive and the fever had subsided. A few hours elapsed and she asked for some gruel.

When Peregrine was satisfied that the invalid would recover fully, he departed again for Marningham Hall, thanking God that his prayers had been answered.

Baskerville Hall

The Ball

CHAPTER SEVEN

PEREGRINE GOES TO LONDON

Six months elapsed, during which time Peregrine had to attend to his farms, and address the problems of his tenants, before he could leave for London. His all important mission was to find out from Sir John the reason for Lucy's rejection of his proposal. He felt sure that Sir John would be able to answer the question, and so he set out on the arduous journey, arriving eventually at the Fanshawe Club, where he was to spend the night. The following day he had arranged to lunch with Sir John at the House of Commons. The House in those days, was a bastion of male company, long before women could become Members, and so he found the dining room full of men, chattering about politics and other matters. He made for Sir John, seated in the far corner of the room.

'My dear good fellow, how are you!' exclaimed Sir John, not waiting for an answer but launching into an account of the current debates in the House.

Soon they were engaged in earnest conversation while eating their meal. At the end of lunch Peregrine broached the reason for his visit.

'I have come to London specially to see you in person,' he said. 'I wanted to ascertain the reason why Lucy has rejected my proposal of marriage.'

Sir John, of course, had been asked some time ago for the hand of his daughter in marriage and had gladly consented, since he thought highly of his prospective son-in-law.

However, he was not prepared to divulge the reason, preferring to leave it to Lucy.

'I think you will have to ask her the reason yourself,' he said.

With that the matter was dropped and for the rest of lunch other topics were discussed.

Peregrine returned to Lincolnshire with the question still unanswered. He knew that some other means would have to be found for discovering the reason and no doubt, in due course, he would be told.

CHAPTER EIGHT

THE DARK DISCOVERY AND
THE TRUTH WILL OUT

Our hero did not have long to wait for the reason for the rejection of his proposal. He was entertaining friends to tea in the drawing room one day when Carter entered with a message for him. Lucy had written to say that she wished to see him, to reveal the reasons for her refusal of his proposal but that she had to tell him in person. He despatched his valet to prepare his clothes. Soon he was ready and, with his valet sitting behind on the dickie, once more set off for Baskerville Hall.

As the carriage sped through the countryside, he observed the corn ripening in the fields and the hedgerows filled with the grey tufts of old man's beard- a sure sign that autumn had arrived. It was with a sense of eager anticipation that Peregrine awaited the revelation that he had wanted for so long. They drove through the night and only stopped briefly on the second night, and by early evening they had reached the Hall.

'Peregrine,' said Lucy. 'Do sit down. You must be very weary after your journey. I will order some refreshment to be brought to you.'

Once the refreshment had arrived she began to talk.

'It is not for personal reasons that I cannot marry you. It is because I have an invalid brother and I am his keeper. He has a deformity in his legs and cannot walk properly, and although he has a nursemaid called Daisy, I mean everything to him and I could not leave him.'

Peregrine drew a deep breath. So that was it. The child he had seen that day when he had opened the door to the nursery was Lucy's brother, for whom she was proposing to sacrifice her entire life. What a loyal person she was.

'I understand the situation completely,' he

said. 'You must do what you think best. Let me ponder on the problem awhile.'

The solution to the problem did not immediately occur to him, and it was only after he returned to Lincolnshire that he had decided that the answer should be, whatever the consequences, that Edmund, the invalid boy, should come and live with them at Marningham Hall.

Lucy was delighted of course, and once more Peregrine found himself on bended knee with the ring in his pocket, asking his beloved's hand in marriage. His proposal accepted, the couple fixed a date for their marriage, which took place three months later in the tiny church at the bottom of the drive, with Edmund present to see his sister take her vows, dressed in the most exquisite ivory satin gown sewn with a myriad of seed pearls and heavily embroidered with coloured silks. Afterwards the party repaired to the house to drink a toast to the happy couple before they went away on their honeymoon.

They had decided not to go far afield for their honeymoon because of Edmund, just to a small house on the estate of some friends nearby. There they talked and walked and hatched plans for their future, and Peregrine told Lucy that he would buy her a thoroughbred horse for her wedding gift, so that they could go riding together. Everything boded well as they set off for their matrimonial home, Marningham Hall in the county of Lincolnshire in the fifteenth day of April, 1793.

PART 2

CHAPTER NINE

LUCY ANSTRUTHER – MISTRESS OF MARNINGHAM HALL

Lucy, in real life became the Viscountess Jervis, a title bringing her an elevated status, which made her a prominent figure in the County. She was invited to open fêtes, attend galas and balls and, as Lord Anstruther's wife, generally became a leading figure in Society. This position, however, did not satisfy our heroine and she sought some other means of fulfilling her life as a virtuous woman. Had not her father shown her that there was more to life than just attending balls and parties? There was little for her to attend to in the house, for Peregrine wished to continue overseeing the housekeeping, having a meeting with the housekeeper each morning to decide on the menus and other household matters.

'Dearest,' said Lucy one day when they were

out riding. 'I am very happy here, but I wish to fulfil a lifelong desire to do some good in the wider world. I have the intention of approaching Cloudsley House, a home for fallen women, to see if I can be of some help there.'

Peregrine looked aghast, and lost no time in expressing his feelings.

'Can you really think that a woman in your position can go amongst such women?' he asked incredulously.

'It is in my position that I feel I can help by visiting these poor creatures,' she explained. 'I have approached the vicar you know, to ask him his advice, and he has suggested Cloudsley because it is not too far away, and is in need of help.'

'I cannot allow you to do such a thing,' Peregrine declared, by this time in a state of frenzy. After much persuasion he relented and said she was to go there once but no more.

So it was that, the following Wednesday, accompanied by her sister Jessica, who had been staying with them, she ordered the carriage for two o'clock in the afternoon to go into Lincoln.

Cloudsley House was a Georgian building situated on an eminence on the outskirts of the city. From its elevated site, Lucy beheld a panoramic view of the city, with the cathedral in the distance.

The housekeeper answered the door, and showed the two women into an anteroom where some half a dozen women were gathered. At first they were so overawed by the presence of such elevated company that they remained silent as Lucy spoke encouraging words to each of them in turn. She then bade them farewell, saying that she would visit them the following week. First of all, of course, she had to persuade Peregrine that her weekly visits were worth while, and that they would in no way detract from her position in the county.

The following week, having persuaded her reluctant husband that she would come to no harm,, she visited the home again, and ascertained that there was an acute shortage of clothes amongst the women. Her mission was therefore to persuade her friends to part with some of their vast wardrobe of elegant garments. She introduced the subject when she was entertaining several of them to tea one day in the drawing room.

'If you have any clothes that you no longer want,' she began hesitantly. 'I will gladly take them off you.'

'What for?' asked one of the women suspiciously.

'Because they are needed at Cloudsley House,' replied Lucy.

'Cloudsley House!' exclaimed one 'but that is a home for fallen women! Surely you do not go near such a place!'

Prejudice was not lacking in Society, it seemed, but eventually the women agreed to look at their wardrobes to see what could be discarded, and a whole pile was conveyed by the coachman to the home and distributed amongst its occupants, who surely had never seen such finery.

One of the women in the home was Meredith, who had been found by the superintendant one night, cowering in a doorway in the centre of the city with her baby, then barely six months old. Meredith had been offered a place in the home together with her baby, who was called Maud. After visiting the house several times Lucy offered her the vacant post of scullery maid at the Hall.

Lucy invited Meredith to visit the Hall for the purpose of discussing her employment and meeting the other servants. She was taken to the kitchen, with its huge copper pans adorning the walls and long table in the centre, with its range (an old fashioned version of the Aga today), —

and the scullery on the floor below, as well as the stillrooms where chutneys and jams were made. Meredith, who had never seen such a range of implements used by any cook, was amazed by what she saw. Of course this was well before the age of refrigeration, so meat was kept cool in the larder. The green baize door, she learnt, separated the kitchen with its unsavoury odours from the main part of the house. Above all, Meredith noticed the formal address of the servants towards their ladyship the Viscountess Anstruther. How would she settle in to this strictly run community and hierarchy she wondered?

In a household such as this a servant would rise at 6.30 every morning, do the breakfasts, wash the dishes then make the beds. After that she would clean up the washstands, fill the waterjugs, then sweep and dust the bedrooms; attend to the candlesticks and put everything in perfect order in the sitting rooms. From 11 o'clock to 3 o'clock she would turn out one or two of the rooms and eat her dinner in the meantime, at 4 o'clock she was to put on a clean cap and apron. Then she would get the servants' afternoon tea and clear it away. After that she would fill up the time until supper with needlework. Finally she was to make a round of the rooms and sew until quarter past ten.

CHAPTER TEN

MAUD

Lucy soon spotted that Maud had above average intelligence, and engaged a tutor for her, just as she had for her own children. Maud quickly learnt to read, and read not soft covered books but hard covered ones with small print. Eventually Maud was ready to go out into the world and wished to become a governess, which was one of the few occupations then open to women. Unfortunately, there being no colleges for governesses nearby, Maud was taken on at the Hall to serve as a house parlourmaid, along with her mother, who had been employed there for three years.

At lunch in the servants' hall one day, she had made the acquaintance of a steward named Jack. Jack had immediately taken a fancy to the young girl, who was becoming a handsome lass with her flaxen curls done up with blue ribbon, and asked her to walk down to the town with him that afternoon.

Maud agreed, pleased to acquire her first boy friend. At that time Jack had little money and no prospects, and was in no position to ask any girl to marry him. Eventually he acquired a new post elsewhere as a butler with better wages and more prospects. He hatched a plan, that he would ask Maud to move to the new position with him and that they should get married. Maud agreed, for, to tell the honest truth, she felt she had little hope of ever getting married, and certainly not to someone with prospects. Had she trained to be a governess she recognised that it was unlikely, in her position of social isolation, that she would ever meet anyone to marry. She thus accepted Jack's proposal and they were married in the local parish church.

One day Jack asked her about her father.

'I do not know who my father was,' she replied truthfully. Her mother had become pregnant with Maud while she was a prostitute and had no means of tracing the father. All she knew was that he was of a good family.

Jack suggested that she should try and trace him, but the search proved fruitless and he had to be satisfied that she had some good stock in her veins.

CHAPTER ELEVEN

THE END OF THE STORY

And so the story ends, a tale which I hope gives a portrait of a colourful age, an age of elegant clothes and sumptuous food, an age of intrigue and romance and of strong relationships, of balls, parties and dinners and of high living for the wealthy at least. For the poor, however, it was a life of grinding poverty, such as one reads about in novels,. Women were not able to vote until the beginning of the twentieth century, the railway age had not yet dawned, and the motor car was an invention well into the future. It was an age before bathrooms, lavatories and personal hygiene. It is a matter for debate whether one would prefer to live then or in the present day.

Fortunately at least, there is a plethora of literature, both written in the eighteenth century and at the present time, to tell us more about this fascinating time.

The End

SOURCES AND SELECT BIBLIOGRAPHY

The internet. Life in the eighteenth century. (Costume dept. of the V and A.)

BOOKS (including selected reading on the eighteenth century).

Women in England – a Social History. 1760-1914, by Susie Steinbach.

English Country Life in the Eighteenth Century. 1780-1830 by E.W. Bovill.

Mistress of the House. Great Ladies and Grand Houses 1670-1830 by Rosemary Baird.

Regency Design 1790-1840 by John Morley

Life in the English Country House by Mark Girouard.

English Social History by George Trevelyan.

Architecture in Britain 1500-1830 by John Summerson.

The Grand Tour. The lure of Italy in the eighteenth century by Andrew Wilton.

DIARIES

Diaries of Maria Edgeworth.

ART

Eighteenth century paintings by artists Joshua Reynolds, Thomas Gainsborough and Arthur Devis.

For information on costumes.

NATIONAL PORTRAIT GALLERY. Relevant eigtheenth century paintings.

Lightning Source UK Ltd.
Milton Keynes UK
UKOW05f0738200614

233777UK00001B/1/P

9 781783 060252